Let's Brush Our Teeth!

Adapted by Alexandra Cassel Schwartz
Poses and layouts by Jason Fruchter

SIMON SPOTLIGHT

An imprint of Simon & Schuster Children's Publishing Division • New York London Toronto Sydney New Delhi
1230 Avenue of the Americas, New York, New York 10020 • This Simon Spotlight edition May 2021
For more information about special discounts for bulk purchases, please contact Simon & Schuster Special Sales
at 1-866-506-1949 or business@simonandschuster.com. • Manufactured in the United States of America 0321 LAK
1 2 3 4 5 6 7 8 9 10 • ISBN 978-1-5344-8534-1

Good morning, neighbor! It's a beautiful day.
Let's brush our teeth before we play.

Grab your toothbrush and come along.
Brushing keeps our teeth clean and strong!

Carefully remove the toothbrush from the back of the book.

Mom squeezes toothpaste onto the brush.
It's the one that Daniel likes so much!

Carefully remove the toothpaste from the back of the book.

♪ *Then you brush the bottom teeth, the bottom teeth!* ♪
Brush the bottom and make sure that you've got them!

Use the toothbrush to brush Daniel's bottom teeth from side to side.

♪ Then you brush the front teeth. Brush the front teeth! ♪
Make little circles and open up wide!

Make little circles with the toothbrush to brush
the front of Daniel's teeth.

Use the toothbrush to brush all the way to the back of Daniel's mouth.

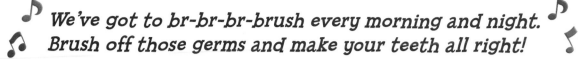

DING!

Put the toothbrush under the faucet to rinse off the toothpaste.

Daniel sips some water and swishes it around.
He spits it back out and puts his toothbrush down.

Then he flosses everywhere in between.
Daniel's teeth feel very smooth and clean!

Carefully remove the floss from the back of the book.
Then help Daniel floss his teeth!

Now Daniel is ready to play, play, play.
And he'll brush again at the end of the day.

Before Daniel goes to bed at night,
he brushes his teeth until they're white.

Now you know how to brush your teeth too.
Thank you for helping. Ugga Mugga to you!